42 DEGREES OF TRUTH

VICTORIA RAY

Contents

Part IV
HAVE I SAID ENOUGH YET? OH, NOT ENOUGH? OK THEN, HOW ABOUT THIS?

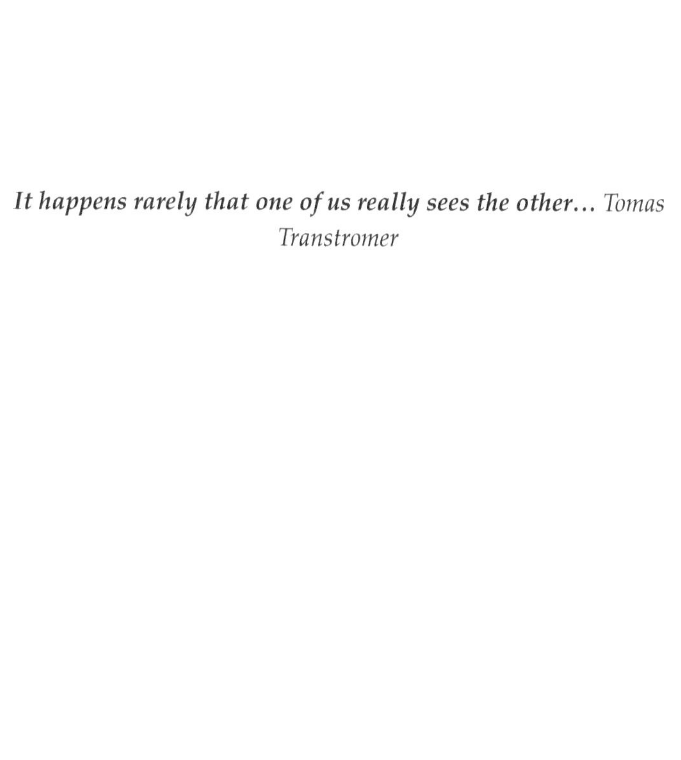

It happens rarely that one of us really sees the other... Tomas Transtromer

<u>FOREWORD</u>

There's no real standard for what makes a good or a bad poem. What matter is – if you feel anything after reading it; if it resonates with your emotions or life situation; if the words swirl in your head for many years afterwards or stay with you for the rest of your life.

The poems in this book are melancholic, symbolic and dark, but at the same time - seriously funny, luminous and vulnerable. They are alive. They transcend you into another world. They discuss social issues. They are meaningful and witty. They are the extension of my soul.

See it more as the story, a concept, a situation, or maybe a dance of words. See it more as satire - directed to expose and criticize; or irony – a difference between appearance and reality.

There's someThing there.

There's someOne there…

Ray

PART I

THE WILD UNKNOWN: PICK A DIRECTION

THE BEGINNING

If you think this book looks like a mess
You are right
But I might warn you
That unfortunately
Mess is the place where we are living
In fact
We don't give a damn
Where, how and why

***

Or if we live at all.

What really makes me sick
Is that we know everything
But continue
Rolling in the garbage.

It goes on
And on
And on
For way too long.

That's why this book is here
To inform you
that you have entered the last stage.

Inspired by the quote of Hannah Arendt:

> *When all are guilty, no one is; confessions of collective guilt are the best possible safeguard against the discovery of culprits, and the very magnitude of the crime, the best excuse for doing nothing."*

When all are guilty – no one is.
Everybody is the Saint,
with a knife and a hidden smile.
Behind that smile, we'll find
A fear.
With a voice.
It gives the loudest speech
To crime.
But in the noise,
Cannot be heard.
He, she, it – all are deaf.

Well, weak minds have no ears,
they say.
It is believed,
Those,
without a heart… can't hear itself.
What a sad way to spend this life!

When all are guilty – no one is.
Ignorance is talking hatefully to wisdom.
Intentions are very simple:
To keep the wisdom silent,
And sanity – underground.

Successfully done!

Long-haired donkey raised its voice:
"Hey, Johnny, how can I help you?
Oh, Dear!
I would have killed you sooner,
But I had several errands to run.
If you are still interested – next Monday is free.
I'll put you on my list.
Prepare to unzip your soul for me
I've found a cure for your fair heart,
It is called… Slavery."

Black' and 'White' without grey is – "Us".
'You' and 'Me' without Us is – "Dead".

And the color for Two?
Your guess…
Is it color of Love?
More or less.

Why sometimes all I want is blue?
Bleeding nails on the wall of the night…
Maybe blue is nothing but you,
And the walls will fall down seeing the light.

'Black' and 'white' without grey is – "You".
'White' and 'black' without You is – "One".

I don't need to tell you that,
You knew.
And the next, our color?
'The Sun'.

Silence.
There's someone in my room,
Sitting and staring.
Maybe it's just the air,
Maybe it's just the waves of my fear.
What's the difference?
Zero.
Either way:
There's someone in my room,
Sitting and staring.

I can smell the darkness
Throwing its arrow across my bed.
The darkness is my matchless friend.

It's burning hot here.
The house is screaming
Like a villain from the movies,
With a really bad moustache,
Forever requesting blood,
Ready for battle,
Burned to ash.

I stare into infinity.
Wondering...
If there's someone out there
Who really cares?
And then I ask the darkness:
'Where's my tea?'

   I'm not good at playing a victim.

     If a beer inside of me could talk...

I know you "Can"!
Just try to hold it tighter,
Yes, T-I-G-H-T-E-R!
Pretend that you are looking at the stars.
Of course, it's a rainy day, dumbass.
That's why it is a good idea!

    Police are here. Fuck MY LIFE!
    I mean your 'life' as well.
    We are forever bound, my hero.
    Explain to me –
    Why they never sleep?
    Too cold – they are outside!
    Too hot – they are outside!
    'Outside' is their lifestyle.
    Don't they hate it? Ever?

      Tell them that you are drinkin'
      Sprite or Coca-Cola
      Yes, there're such beverages,
      At the bars as well.
      And yes, you are alone.
      Take off your hands from Willy.
      Immediately!
      Well done.

Good boy...
Find something else to hold.
No, not a belly.
And not *me*. I wanna be 'incognito'.
At least for once!
If this is even possible with you.

Ok. Next step – big smile. Try it.
Don't be stupid.
Oh no, noooooo!!!!
NOOOOOO! NO, NO, NO!
What's that scared look for?
Stand still.
Let me listen.
Aha!
They are asking what are you doing here:
In the darkness, outside of an empty school?
Hm.

Tell them you are the local teacher,
And you forgot your laptop in the classroom.
Don't try to get inside the school
through that cracked dirty window.
You are the teacher! AKA smart!
Please, stop shouting like a feeble-minded fuck!
Follow my lead – I'll keep you out of trouble.

And stop singing!
I can't think with your drunk voice around me.
Oh, don't breathe in it!
They'll throw you in the jail.
For what?
Because you love me, Silly man!

...like the river flows
flows the happiness
through my hands
every day.

Every step we take
Makes the Earth less alive,
Breaks her down.
Are we evil? Tell me.
Are we evil, people?

Evil is the wound.
Acne. The pain.
You can't scrub it away.
You CAN'T scrub it away.
Away of everything,
Or over and over. Again.
You'll be hunted in the darkness,
– falling.

Hunted in the darkness
Between paralyzed dreams
And overwhelmed wishes.
Staring at your own reflection,
– feeding.

Staring at the reflection
Of never-ending promises,
that were once yours.
And the wings
Spinning slowly,
losing everything,
even… the air,
– *pleading.*

I wish I could hear
Like the river flows
Every day.

Every day
through my hands
flows the happiness…

"I can
almost understand
why
people
leap
from
bridges..."
Said Bukowski about November.

Ray: WAY. TOO. NICE.

Bukowski: I'm glad you noticed that, Ray!

Ray: I'm an expert in swearing, bridges and Novembers.

Bukowski: Damn, what about popcorn and buzz?

Ray: I'm a very dedicated fan of popcorn and almost untouchable by buzz. ALMOST.

Bukowski: Ray, you are nice today. Much nicer than yesterday. I mean, almost worth my attention.

Ray: Frankly, I was horrified that you forgot that I visited you yesterday...

Bukowski: Yesterday? Did you?

Ray:

I wish you
Luck
With your memory.
Or
Maybe
It is November -
Senseless Hell
Of foggy sheets,
Drinking my blood.
But it's still nice —
to live.

Real poem:

"Draw me a poem, –
said the voice in my head.
Draw me some love,
neck to neck on the bed".

The thoughts of a poet:
I'd like to say
just throw me the last Playboy,
if you wanna make an ol' boy happy.
And yes, I'm hungry for dat Love.
Long-time no see.
Last time I slept neck to neck
in my bed with someone?
Oh, sweet memories.
It was with Winnie.
Yes, The Pooh. My favorite.
He made me cry.
Whatever.
Let's continue.

Real poem:

2. "Give me hot passion,
through the pair of eyes,
Give me a stranger –
with a pocket of smiles."

Aha!

Real poem:

*3. "Draw me a girl –
said the stranger to me.
Draw me her voice,
singing love to the sea".*

Oho!

Real poem:

4. "I can't forget

the voice of that girl.
And the beauty-sunset,
That shines like a pearl."

Wow!

The thoughts of a poet:
Ok. I've messed up 'the ending'.
But who cares about the sunset or 'shine'?
Where is the logic?
If the girl has *an ass*
that can stop traffic…
Well, that's all that matters.

Real poem:
5. "Let every day
be the day of Love.
Let every heart
See the doves from above."

The thoughts of a poet:
Started dreaming about everything I wrote above, but then, I
got very depressed all of a sudden…

<u>A Girl In A Black Box</u>

Inspired by the book "Negroland", Margo Jefferson.

There's a girl in a black box.
The man asks her: What are you doing here?
She says: I don't know. But thank you for noticing me.

Next morning, he tells his wife
About the girl in the black box.
She shrugs: "Why do you care?"
"Because she's *me,*" he responds with a worried look.

In the evening, the box is surrounded by people.
Peopled people.
Those
who never lived in the box.
They talk loudly about the girl.
Like she is not there,
listening,
watching,
each of their movement.
Ready...
To be invited to the conversation.

"The box isn't the issue," says one.
"The girl should stay where she belongs!" says another.
"I have a raffle," says the third.

"Goodnight. Sweet dreams, people," -
the girl is tired from the loud voices.
The crowd is frozen:
'How dare you?'

There's an empty black box on the street.
It is still black.
Just like everything around us.

Inspired by Freddy Kreuger – *a character from the A Nightmare on Elm Street film series.*

I know, hun, I know you are outside
In that cold old phone booth
Waiting for help to arrive
Hands are shaking, and tears are
Running in the dark solitude
But you can NOT hide from me, baby,
No way. You can NOT hide.

I can smell it, your fear of death,
That beautiful shock in your eyes
You are ready to fight, l'il Faust
Go ahead; I am two breaths away,
On the edge of the last…
Yes, of course, hun, you will survive
No doubt, you will do, my baby dust.

Almost there
Almost done
Almost the end

Life is a coward, cold despair, my girl,
Don't believe me? Oh, wait!
Let me show it to you, my mystery pearl.

Always here
Always ready
To kill in full swing

Life is a coward, cold despair, my girl,
Let me show it to you… - *Every Thing*.

Arched body, legs up
A little faster this time -
'Flexing' into you.

Finger yourself more
While I'm writing a love poem
On your naughty breasts.

Going deep. Slowly.
In love all over again
with your 'tight wet scream'.

Imagine how great
To move from the floor to the counter
With my tongue on your clit.

"Squeeze me," your breast said.
Hungry. My tongue is intense -
Enjoying *the last meal*.

On your hand and knees,
Pushing my balls in circles...
That's how I want you.

I'm so bad at this...
Let's watch Star Wars and get high.
Don't beg! I'm soft.

<u>I'D STILL SWIM</u>

Inspired by Abraham H. Maslow:

If I were dropped out of a plane into the ocean and told the nearest land was a thousand miles away, I'd still swim. And I'd despise the one who gave up."

I'd still swim to you...
To my dazzling shore of hope,
To my heart-racing wave of a tale,
To the depth I never seen before,
To the 'bad blood cut'.
My prison at dawn,
My sweetest 'apricot'

I wouldn't fear all 'mistakes'
You've done.
To steal the sun and hide it in your pocket,
To stalk my dreams while wearing 'clown mask',
To drink my bitter coffee
Or
To guide my feet into the shoes each morning.
My music of the falling leaves,
My Miss 'Divine Tobacco'.

I'd still swim to you...
Through the smashed sea of salt,
Through fire, curved in the row of dancing birds.
Or under water,
Both hands into the burning sand.
I would still swim.

I would.
I will.

I would.
BUT NOT TODAY!
Too tired.
And seems, sweet darling,
You are still a thousand miles away…

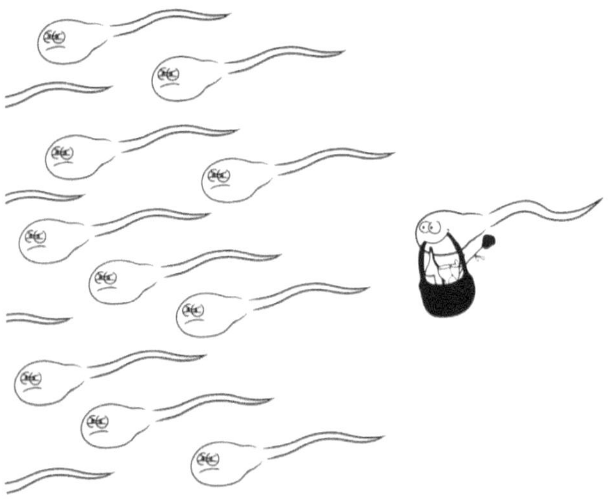

PART II

THE ROOTS OF MORALITY

Another restless night.
A room with a single bed.
Butterflies are singing:
Wake up!
On the couch and in my head,
Giving me hope that anything is possible.

Mr Tequila came in,
Hugged me,
Until I sank into my slumber,
Completely gone.
Disappeared like the wind.

"You didn't answer my call",
I whispered.
"No, I didn't, Miss Maybe.
Because you are dead…"

I took a deep breath,
Picked up my life from the floor -
Ready to go.
"I am leaving. See you soon, Mr Tequila."
"Don't worry; you can't go anywhere. Maybe… later?"

I decided to learn to fly.
Unexpectedly slipped,
Whipped out the traces of
Vomit from the blouse.

"Is everything all right?"
Mr Tequila asked, arriving

Like a ghost from nowhere.

"Maybe. Or maybe not.
Oh, Tequila …
Nothing can be truly fun
Without you!"

Pain is streaming down my face.

"I love you," he said,
And closed the grave.

That love felt good on my skin.
I wanted to ask him –
Why, why am I *here*, if you really love me?
But I didn't. Instead, I stared from the other side, through the
stone of granite, mesmerised by the silent synchronization of
his hand, writing:

"What the hell? How is it even possible?" I thought… A large cup of coffee waited on the table – an absolute joy after the dark, riddled dream.

You don't know me.
You are too far to see my sins
Too numb to fight the freezing clouds
Too cold to turn my heart into an arrow.
You are a wild rain or a rumble of thunder.
You are everything around me,
All people on the earth…
Gone,
But still here.
Laughing at my pain,
Haunting my shadows
Inside of a broken mirror
Into which I stare every day.

I drag myself deeper in
To try to get to you.
To say - my room is lonely.
No hope.
All is fear.
I breathe my soul down your throat…
But you don't know me.

I feel I'm losing it.
The World.
And You.
And All.

<u>**ONCE IN HAVANA**</u>

Inspired by the book 'Next Year in Havana', Chanel Cleeton

There was a girl
who came to Havana
and met Luis,
almost married.

She peered over his shoulder
and saw that there's no freedom
in Cuba.
Not yet.

None of the things you own is yours.
The framed photographs on the wall
Have witnessed mad La Cabana-sex.
Just once.
Not too much
to be sad
if you'll cross paths again.

Paths with real, hot, non-luxury Luis
that would not have been crossed,
If she'd be one happy beach gal.

Are you ready to shake Cuba up and down?
To spill the truth over the living world?

Oh, girl, it could work in Florida, but here,
Fidel is still a Curse of Everything,
Fidel is immortal, and he doesn't like you.
Nothing personal…

The grandma with a guitar

Singing quietly from The Land of Dead:
"For those, involved with my ashes:
Understand –
It wasn't like that in Cuba before,
Pick them all up and go back home!'

'It makes no sense,' whispered the girl from the bed, joining
Luis for one more round...

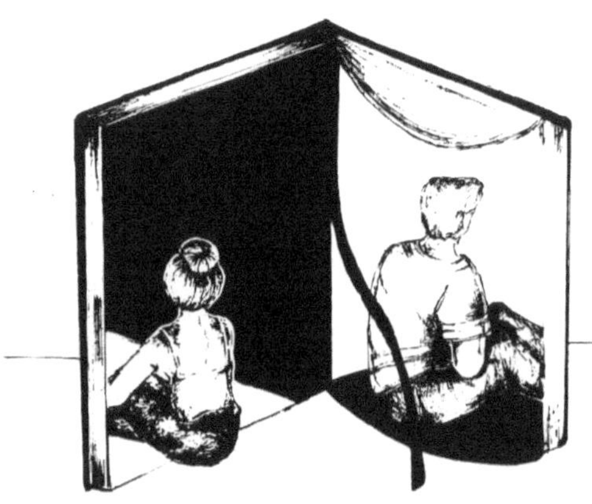

The hand of a human –
On the wheel of the Earth.
Extremely strong,
Yet, weak.
Shaking from the gravity pull,
Looking for a higher purpose,
Travelling between the galaxies,
Deep in thought.
Admiring the layers of stars,
Spilling the dust of hate across the Milky Way…
Breaking lives, freeing poison.
Wishing to dig deeper,
to understand more.

"More" – *what? where? and why?*

No war.
No enemy.
No end.
Only you.

Look around…
You are sitting by the grave.
Read the damn words on the stone:
"I DID NOTHING BUT GOOD."

Loneliness is a phobia
Of big breasts and roads with no end,
The empty plates and plastic bags,
dark ones,
With your name on it.

Loneliness is not Tuesday,
but Wednesday.
Especially if
A Happy Hour
Is taken away,
Forgotten
Because you have to work
For the boss
who doesn't ask shit from you,
But you do it anyway.

Loneliness is a gun
Pointed to your head.
Not somewhere far
But here,
at home,
on the porch.
It is the hollow sound of your wife
Blowing away the dreams
Of the next year together
While hugging the short dick of Joe
With her lips.

Who is Joe?
Why do you care?
Joe is one lonely dude.
Just like you.
Don't worry…
Your life is throwing at you
Only those meetings
that you can handle.

Loneliness is a hashtag
Of words you don't understand
But you want to.
You are dreaming
To become popular
For one month.
A day.
Or one hour.
If ever…
Let's do it again –
push the poor soul of yours
out, ON the LINE.

ᴗᴗᴗ

You are going to your room,
Grabbing a phone
Cutting open your chest
(would be nice to cut open the chest of that Joe, but you are a
coward)
To check
If it is still there -
THE HEART.
To show to the world
"Yes, I am social. I am You."

1 January, 2:25am

We thought it would be fun.
To wear shorts in shiny snow,
To fall asleep with sausage roll
Between the legs.
And let all beer,
Vodka
And Tequila
Sing "Hallelujah" to Japan and back.
To find a three-legged cat without an eye
To chat about a little rain of wine…
For everyone to drink,
Or have a bath.

1 January, 1:13pm

It feels like punishment this morning.
Woke up with smelly feet close to my face.
The feet, you never wanted to touch,
to see,
to act with.
Something,
that reminds me about
the Evil Dead -
hallucinations, or nightmares.
Those darkest
I can't even name…
When all is burning heat,
and rats
worms
evils
start suddenly to dance

flamenco.
Inside your gut.
And you are expecting death.

1 January, 7:21pm

But let's get back to you,
who pushed me
to write these passionate 'confessions'.
You told me
It was the grand finale of the old race,
And we are on the trip to win the New.
New Mind.
New Kama Sutra.
New Mattress.

But all I can remember is
a cake
we bought at a local store.
And how I fed it to a fish we found,
or ate,
or spoke to…hm.
Anyway, tell me,
why was it so significant
to follow neighbours
(or was it their dog?)
until the sunrise.
Why did you try to jump and cry:
"Nurse! Nurse! I am getting worse!"

Oh, never mind.
I understand.
That was important.

2 January, 3:20am

I don't feel my nuts. Feel nothing. What time is it?

2 January, 9am

I'd like to rhyme my thoughts
With a glass of wine
Or beer
Or tequila.
Yes! Again!
Tequila is a new #trend.
Or a friend…
The End.

She's a pretty silver dress
and I'm a dark wool jacket
To keep you warm.
She's a violin
and I'm a raspy tired voice
You never listen to.
She is that funny laughing child
and I'm an old window
in the cold and boring kitchen.
Grey cloud,
forgotten horn of dreams,
The needy hand
Who is always waving at you,
And hoping you'll wave back.
Her smell is a pleasure.
Mine?
The rot of ashes,
A slaughterhouse with dying corners
Or the sunrise without the sky
The ocean that never breaks the waves
The joyless daylight
The fever for your happy Christmas.
I see it in your eyes
Inside of each of your atoms…
Don't lie.
I know.
I'm running out of time.
Time waits for no one.
But let me tell you:
sometimes I feel the presence of the
Goddess inside of me.
The living air, blue sky

Sweet sound of harmony,
Awakening and singing…
And then again –
I see Her in your eyes:

She is your Oz, and I am only Kansas.

IF I ONLY COULD

Draw my face with a chalk
Without name.
Read my lips on the cup
Without shame.
Chase the blood in my veins
Without sound.
Turn your tongue into a knife
Without love.
Give me time to escape,
Break the chains.
Give me a chance to avoid
All mistakes.
Let me find you inside
Of each word.
Let me bring you peace
Without a sword.
I would sell every part
Of my life
If I only could get
Your reply.
I would leave all my worries
In the dust.
If I only could make it all
… last.

There's a space in the darkness.
I can open it, like a bag.
For you.
But I won't.
Because you are the monster,
The evil by nature,
The one,
Who's using the dark in the wrong way.

There's life between sounds.
I can sing it, like a Malaysian frog.
For you.
But I won't.
Because you are the cough,
Deep inside of me,
The one,
Who's pushing the fire out - from the Earth's grave.

There's a 'hole' inside of your ear.
I can jump there: in and out.
For you.
But I won't.
Because you are the smoke
Clouding around me,
The one,
Who's slowing my breath with the fears of doubt.

There's NOTHING inside of you.
Wait.
I can fill it with love.
But I won't...

Pump the blood out...
Let the fury inside of you
destroy the tenderness
of soft and fragile skin.
Take all the fluid you can,
With a bitter sorry smile.
Don't stop your 'hunger.'
On the half-way of the heartbeat.

We don't belong together...
Yes, I know. Because
Your love is like crazy needles
And mine? - The Screaming Kingdom.
I would invite you
Into my strangest dreams,
My fears and desires,
Mind-wire of the pain.
But... are you ready?

Pump the blood out.
You need it more than I do.
Don't stop... Please, don't!
Take all you can — each drop of it.

Mortality is lost, you say.
Oh no!
It's burning like a fire
Each time you hold my hand.
Who are you, dear friend:
White Angel or Emotional Vampire?

"Ray Not Bradbury is next!" the voice arrived.

"Me??" I couldn't recognize my quiet 'squeak'.
The waiting room is full of bright warm red
Ok, let's move inside - for the bloody test.

To really listen…
Is NOT for everybody.
How many times have you played this game -
Dropping the words
Without even noticing the scale of being somewhere else?

To really listen…
Is to SHAKE yourself out of the dream.

To admit the comfort and the presence
Of being on the surface of the Earth,
Here and Now, looking
Into the horizon of a Carpe Diem,
Screaming, from the depths of Infinite
The song of No-Singing.

To really listen…
Is to GET UP and pour a glass of water.

And just sit there,
On the edge of
'Looking for clues'-moment.
Watching,
How the pain is disappearing,
Flying away,
Without explanation.

To really listen...
Is to become a GUARDIAN.

And to seal each bad memory
With the help of your temper,
Or boots...
Or kindness.

You don't know me.
You are too far to see my sins
Too numb to fight the freezing clouds
Too cold to turn my heart into an arrow.
You are a wild rain or a rumble of thunder.
You are everything around me,
All people on the earth…
Gone,
But still here.
Laughing at my pain,
Haunting my shadows
Inside of broken mirror
In which I stare every day.
I drag myself deeper in
To try to get to you.
To tell you that my room is lonely.
No hope.
All is fear.
I breathe my soul down your throat…
But you don't know me.

I feel I'm losing it.
The World.
And you.
And All.

PART III

SOUL SHAKING INSPIRATION

You aren't a hero
God-alike, extra-strong Hercules
You are "an average Joe."
Holding champagne and
Sinking in self-discovery, caffeine and
A blurred haze of memories.
Today you are epic, almost perfect
Tomorrow you are classical
And by the time I finish my poem –
Antique.

You aren't a hero
Until you know the answers -
What my heart desires…

You are *a fish* that can't swim.
Why?
Because.

Because there's no raging ocean.
Not on your side.
Never on your side.

(written in the restaurant, on the napkin)

I would have left you.

If you could only teach me
How to cut the roots of blue
In the town of Melancholy
You have created
Around my drowned love.

I would have left you.

If somebody
Would give me in return
A boat,
To sail in open water,
Dressed in gold and black…
To fly and search for tiny islands
In unborn 'spring-flowing' light.
To breathe the sea,
And paint butterflies,
The laughing doves,
To jump under the skin of Earth
Like it's the last time…

I would have left you.

If I knew
That the green grass I desired
is greener on the other side of the sunset.
And if I knew,
That your Silly Kingdom
Almost crumbled
In a million of 'winter-cries.'

…and we are on the ground.
Between the fists of edgy fury
And broken Paradise.
Swimming,
In the 'gargles' of Unknown.

I would have left you.

BUT I have no power
To change my appetite.
I want my apple-pie – you know…

Early spring. Escape.
A single, sexy girl in bikini -
Loud complain.

His money disagrees.
Irritation grows between them.
'One cocky bitch,' he sighs

Shaky lips. Desire expands.
The melting sunset smiles.
Already naked. Look!

Bikini on the ground.
Chemical reaction fails.
No doubt. She is a man!

Feeling betrayed.
What the fuck is going on?
Vacation mode is off.

Alone. Cold bed. He screams.
Ah, only a sad, ugly dream.
Perhaps next time…

SHOW ME A SANE MAN

Show me 'a sane man'.
Fool me.
Close my eyes.
Run to a bright light,
Whisper frosting words,
Control and melt my dreams,
My tired soul,
Hide a thousand masks
In quiet move.
Scream immortality
Against the sharpest rocks,
And grasp in sorrow.
Float in ecstasy
Of drunken fireworks.
Then... – stop.
Let spirit stand aside.
And raise the crown of madness,
Unseen by human eyes.

Or maybe...

Jump in the warmth of morning-mellow Sun.
Be glorious and scary,
Like day and night.
Be still.
Be soft.
Like tiny fingers
Of the children,
Or petals of flowers
Stretching to the sun.
And smile.
One million smiles.
Forever smile

With hidden shades of grins
Or cries.
Bleed through your skin,
While we believe your lies…

Show me 'a sane man'!
Fool me.
BE. MY. GUEST.

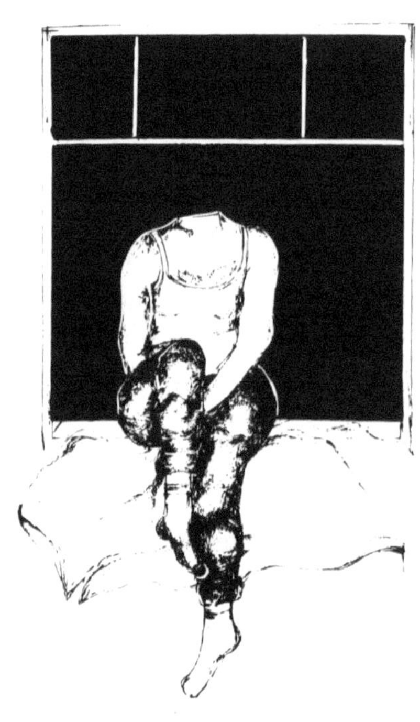

Is it easy – to move the earth?
It's hard to tell.
Often, the heaviest things are the best to float.
Dust. Grains. Stones. Air. Tears of rain.
And light.
Hidden deeply
Among the unborn wall of stars.
Melting the moon every morning.
And stretching a cosmic design.

So alive.

Darkness is watching,
Gazing out of the galaxy-window,
Sitting on my lonely bed,
Pinning me down to the sleep,
Tracking my silence,
Striking the horizon,
Hugging my dreams
With a blanket.
Fills every sound
With love
And infinity.

The Infinity of Weightless Happiness.

Everybody is crying
about love,
about lost or super 'Valentines'.
Everybody wants to be
the one,
to find the one,
become the one,
to be shaped like 'the one'.
To be a slave.
Again.
Everybody is screaming
how they are sad –
ah, the love is gone.
The love is gone forever.
Everybody is wearing
a fake smile on the outside.
Keeping behind closed curtains
Big Hollow space of broken heart.
Empty souls are
searching the heartless crowds:
"Are you there? I am waiting".
And finding zero.
Buried inside of hello's
and goodbye's.
Chewing the pain with the tears.
Trying to find the reason,
to move forward – to the truth…
Trying,
but can't,
at last, for themselves
explain the illusion of "why".

Why?

Because even the endless ocean
has its end, dear.

Why?

Because you are a believer in "maybe".
Let me find it for you
in the country of "Never".

Everybody is praising the love.
Everybody.
But not me.
Sitting in my chair.
Understanding "nothing".

'Nightmare' is a noun.
No legs
to take a walk.
No hands
to hug you tighter.
No dreams
to share on the shelves.
No fantasy
to sparkle on the sheets.
Nightmare is a noun
Of nothing,
But a fear.

'To fear' is a verb.
And when a verb is real,
It might burn down your life,
Or kneel,
Or kill,
Or chew you,
... as a tasty meal.

HO – HO – HO!
GOT YOU!

You are sitting
And telling me,
That you had no idea
What kind of a parasite
Is buried
Under his skin –
Your damn husband.

Husband with a soft voice
But hot temper.
Modern, clean, almost present,
The future of humanity.
In reality –
A smart machine
And a senseless beast.

How ignorant
And egoistical
He is.

Yes, you seduced him with your soft hands, Amazon-a-like hips and curly dark hair in the wrong places. You thought his sweat was a blessing, a sign of love, full of everything a girl needs - romantic pain and burning desires – instead, you are left with a broken squeaky duck, — that how your heart sounds.

Ravaged. Dirty. Ill.

"Never again," you said.

No, you aren't willing to go back.
You have no wish to see your dreams in chains.

A phone call from your husband.
You are answering.
"What should I make for dinner tonight?" you are asking all
of a sudden. This topic is covering everything, even broken
relationships.

GRAVESTONE

Here lies your heart
Blind and holy
In the jaws of Time
Slowly collapsing
Into the dark matter
Of a 'Milky Way'… candy bar.

<u>Legs</u>

Here they are:

Nylon-clad,
Restless,
Swollen,
Sleek,
Unshaven,
Weather-beaten
And flabby.

Beefy,
Aching,
Hunky,
Sturdy,
Misshapen,
Fish-netted
And lumpy.

Energetic,
Naked,
Exhausted,
Tender,
Stained…

But always ready,
To make your dreams come true.

Heart-aching
Nose-itching
Mind-centering

Stressing out,
Fingers and eyes
In the middle of an incredible stillness,
Making out with your phone.

BOOM!

It feels good again.
Wi-Fi makes you relaxed
And focused
Focus makes you alert enough
to notice me…

Sitting across the table
With my face up to the sun
OPEN
To start conversation.

PART IV

HAVE I SAID ENOUGH YET? OH, NOT ENOUGH? OK THEN, HOW ABOUT THIS?

Mirror

'I want to be wanted more than anything else in the world,' someone has whispered from the mirror. It couldn't be me, or could it?

Everything in the world is the reflection of our consciousness. There is no escape from the reality we create. Days and nights pass. Ambitions bloom. Expectations tear the soul apart. We all are consumed by the desire to be the best. The best face. The best personality. The best human. We are too perfect. But still, too empty. We are mirrors without the reflection... lost in time. Lost in fear.

'What does a mirror look at?' someone has whispered back to my face.

It couldn't be me, or could it?

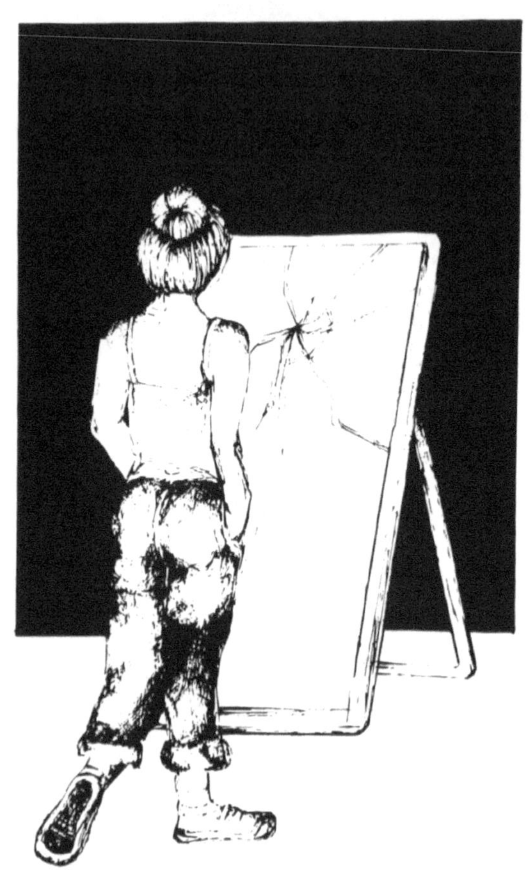

YOU HAVE NOTHING MORE TO GIVE

Inspired by Mary Wollstonecraft:

I never wanted but your heart – that gone, you
have nothing more to give."

You have nothing more to give...

You are an empty spoon.
For everyone who's hungry,
And shadows growing on their faces.
You are a half-nothing at the bar across the street.
For everyone with a hangover
Or thirsty with a fit of anger.
You are a two-words-letter.
For those who are one thousand miles
away from home
too lonely and scared.
You are the pain in chest.
For everyone in the middle of a breakup,
Bruised and bleeding.
You are the summer. Cold and wet.
For every bird,
Who's freezing, but still singing
The Song of Love.

Yes.
You have nothing more to give...

You are the cage.
For everyone who never looked up,
Because their hearts are blind.

It destroys everything around, except itself.
It satisfies its own needs before anything else.
It is on the mission, do not try to distract.
It fears the reality, so it builds a new one.
It is God-a-like, emotionless and non-sexual.
Or over-sexual?

It grows a Genius that feeds on its own importance.
It is in the constant hunger to become a perfect reflection.
Of the World?

It is a mediocre confidence that no-one is enough, but me.
It is the centre of the Universe, that is never satisfied.
It shines with arrogance on the forehead.
Especially when smiling.

It does whatever it takes to feel 'absolute'.
It is shallow and false, addictive and aggressive.
Or simply stupid?

It is his own Creator, filled with envy and emptiness.

<u>The Worms</u>

Inspired by Charles Bukowski *"Burning in water. Drowning in flame."*

I sit among the worms.
Telling myself: this world is upside down.
And tomorrow
When I wake up
Everything that stinks and crawls inside of my head
Will die.

I sit and wait.

My heart is hanging from my mouth for so long
It has forgotten how to behave when the hunger begins, and
the sorrow eats you up. Just disturbing, you know…

The clock is ticking.
The brains are jamming against my teeth, screaming "Let me
out, you are broke, stupid and ugly! Like a paper cup of
coffee, wet and empty. I don't need you!"

I don't need you.
I don't need you…
I don't need you!

I sing those words
For the first time in my life
While standing behind a curtain, hiding, smoking a cigar and
thinking about my sad life, the Virgin Mary, and that old
Ford.

Why?
I ain't a Sinatra.

Maybe because the world is
Unloved.
Suicidal.
Frightened…
By us.

I sit in the cold light
Wondering: how to end this bullshit
And also
How to get drunk and punch every *'body'* I'll meet today in
the face
Make them *burn, burn, burn…*

Especially a postman,
And a dentist,
Ah, and of course, that damn fly.
Because, well… they deserve it.

It's sick, you know,
To die at 2 PM, with a beer
And the view of her warm ass on a flopping mattress,
surrounded by cheap dreams, sweating while fighting the
sheets.

I wish I could kill them – the worms.
Or sell.
Or give as a gift.

But I see you got your own…

No light
No love
No hope
No laughter
Nothing to remember
Only the worms…

Thank God, none of them knows that I am still alive.

And then Ray said:

Bring me 'hope'. Hope is a combination of the empty brain and a woman's heart. It has a purpose. To save you. But instead, it kills each wrecked silence of your soul because Hope is horny, scared and lazy. Just as you are.

Bring me 'love'. Love is a fucking mess. A combination of chemicals and shallow hugs (add pain and pleasure). It likes vendetta. Or a shark-blow-job. True love starts with the heat. And then dies…a few nights later. Leaves your ironed out heart on a Canadian football field.

Bring me 'kindness'. Kindness is a combination of strip poker and social nourishment. It leaks the acid right out of you. Slowly. A powerful tool to save the world. Mercifully smiling. It always cares until it doesn't.

Bring me 'happiness'. Happiness is a combination of silk and a running Brazilian boy. Not all who can run are happy equally. But if you will wait a billion years - evolution will offer you a better brain.

Bring me 'grief'. Grief is weak. A combination of a hungry zombie and speechlessness. A wound in your present. Every fifty seconds, it tries to connect to your wet and hollow 'inside'. But you are asleep, at the wheel.

Bring me 'darkness'. In each of us, there is darkness we don't know — a combination of a full moon, a coffin and deep thinking. The human brain is over fifty per cent darkness. Wow!...What if the darkness is the ultimate cure for all suffering?

Bring me 'light'. Light is Mr Incognito. It is not you, but in your head. A combination of an X-ray of your smile and the wind. From behind the clouds. 'You can do it!' - Light says. Your body nervously steps forward. Poor thing…

Bring me 'God'. God is All and More. A combination of … hm, nobody seems to know the answer.

I don't know why
But every morning
When I am eating my eggs
They are dropping on the floor
Or jumping
From my mouth
Unhappy
About the purpose
I'm giving them.

I don't know why
But every morning
When I'm starting to read
My coffee is getting cold
And it is saying
Straight to my face:
"Social injustice –
This is what It Is".

I don't know why
But every morning
A song is born in my heart
An ugly song
About ungroomed
Over-weight
Wondering 'how the heck it happened.'
Nice country girls
Like Me.

I don't know why
But every morning

The planet is still sizzling
Towards Climate Collapse
It's just a shame
That we are standing
In the middle
And thinking –
That's NOT real.

I don't know why
Stupid people are never shy
Maybe because
Every morning
Their eggs
Are jumping from their mouths
Absolutely happy
In a delusion
That they are omelettes.

I don't know why
But every evening
Women are telling their truths
On the Internet
In hope
Being treated like human beings.
But men are too busy
With the politics
Words
Or movies
About female anatomy.

I don't know why
But every evening
My anxiety is
Raising awareness

In a dead-eyed competition
With my brain
About a proper good night sleep
In years.
A sleep
That's forcing us
To forget
How we all are enjoying
The crawling curiosity
Between debts,
deadlines
And social panics –
Endless good vibes of our reality.

**I don't know why
And who wants to know…**

**"Nevermind" is crushing
On my floor
Just like an egg.**

*Disaster?
You are absolutely right.*

Inspired by John Cage: *I have nothing to say, I am saying it, and that is poetry.*

Sitting in the room,
Reading a book
And eating a sandwich.
One hundred years in the single moment
Passing by…

I see you inside of my sandwich
While I'm still at the floor number thirty,
Comfortably falling,
With a sauce in my pockets.

"It's impossible, what bullshit,"
Said you, smiling.

"I'm from an alternate time-stream,
I can see the future."

"By eating a sandwich?"

If you are afraid – you'd better leave now…
Before you'll discover the world
Where time doesn't move:
No ups or downs.
Go back to your own 'plate'.
Stay there.
Eat your life as quickly as you can.

I woke up – and you are gone.
Still sitting in the room,
Reading a book
And eating a sandwich.
One hundred years passing by…
In one second.

...the bee to make honey, of cow to give milk,
of sun to radiate sunshine, of river to flow".

Voice 1:

I *must confess to you,*
I am the one and only Dhar-,
The key to the Universe.
I am the cosmic order and creation.
I am everything you'll never be.

Voice 2:

Hey, Dhar!
Looking for 'Ma' I've heard?!
If you wanna,
I can shake my booty near your cosmic
Town or bed.
Just give a sign!
I am the One,
Who brings the harmony of Lust
In any ritual - good or bad...
And don't forget - I am preventing Chaos.

Voice 1:

Nope.
Ma is nobody.
Ma is filthy.
The Path to Harmony is Truth.
The Truth is me.
Please, leave me alone, woman!
I am too busy,

I have to check my duties as a King –
The world is sitting in the shit of danger!

Voice 2:

Cha, man!

Accept it!

'Ma' is what makes your whole being so awesome.

To be exactly – even Ka-MA-sutra told me once:

"…THAT was the most amazing "night" I've ever experienced.

Nothing is higher,

When you and all your chakras are dancing on purpose."

Voice 1:

You are U-N-R-E-A-L!

Stop this absurdity!

The source of the existence,

Of love,

Of mind,

Of faith,

IS Dhar!

The Lord of the Divine,

The Light and The Universe!

Voice 3:

Shut up!

You two so-called, "Dhar-Ma."

shouldn't walk around with silly face:

"Look, I am the best!"

Instead, try to reflect –

What satisfies the heart of human?

What do you feel driven to?

What's your devotion?

To give stability and order
to each creature on this planet -
Be good,
be virtuous,
be helpful to others,
be justice,
but bring out happiness,
exist in parallel
of Life and Death… love each other.
Put aside your Ego!
That's how you'll rule the world!

Voice 1 and 2:

And who are you?

Voice 3:

I am Ray.
Creator of this book…

Thank you for reading '42 degrees of truth'. I hope you enjoyed my poems, and it would mean a lot to me if you could leave an honest feedback/review! I appreciate any mention or thoughts about my writing.

If you want to know more about my books, check out my plans for 2020, on my blog – Raynotbradbury on Wordpress.

For info, questions, or collaborations, find me on social media – 'Raynotbradbury' on Goodreads, Instagram or Facebook.

Do not forget to check out my debut book '*So Absurd It Must Be True*' (satire and humor: absurd and bizarre), book #1.

9 789198 560107